MW01046635

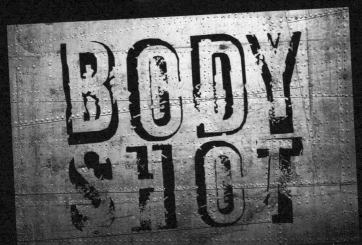

BODY SHOT

BY PATRICK JONES

darbycreek

MINNEAPOLIS

Darby Creek
A division of Lerner Publishing Group, Inc.
241 First Avenue North
Minneapolis, MN 55401 U.S.A.

Website address: www.lernerbooks.com

The images in this book are used with the permission of: © Josh Holmberg/
Cal Sport Media/CORBIS (fighters); © iStockphoto.com/Tim Messick
(background); © iStockphoto.com/Erkki Makkonen (metal wires);
© iStockphoto.com/TommL (punching fist), © iStockphoto.com/dem10
(barbed wire).

Main body text set in Janson Text LT Std 12/17.5.
Typeface provided by Linotype AG.

Jones, Patrick, 1961–
    Body shot / by Patrick Jones.
        pages   cm. — (The dojo ; #4)
    ISBN 978-1-4677-0633-9 (lib. bdg. : alk. paper)
    ISBN 978-1-4677-1634-5 (eBook)
    [1. Mixed martial arts—Fiction. 2. Family problems—Fiction.
3. Drug abuse—Fiction.] I. Title.
PZ7.J7242Cl 2013
[Fic]—dc23   2012042248

Manufactured in the United States of America
1 – SB – 7/15/13

IN MEMORY OF
MILES KLEIN
-P.J.

WELCOME TO THE DOJO

If you're already a fan of mixed martial arts, in particular the Ultimate Fighting Championship (UFC), then you're probably familiar with moves like triangle choke, spinning heel kick, and Kimura. If not, check out the MMA terms and weight classes in the back of the book. You can also go online for videos of famous fights and training videos. Amateur fights are similar to the pros but require more protection for the fighters. While there are unified rules, each state allows for variation.

WELCOME TO THE DOJO.

STEP INSIDE.

CHAPTER 1

"Protect yourself, Meghan!" Mr. Hodge yelled.

Meghan blinked furiously as sweat trickled down. It rested in the tangle of scars on her face before running down to her chin, which was throbbing from Mika's right jab.

Meghan responded with a hard kick to Mika's right side. Even with the thick sparring helmet on, Meghan thought she heard a slight cracking sound, though she was unsure if it was her ankle or Mika's ribs. Meghan felt a little pain, but that wasn't unusual.

"Keep your chin tucked!" Nong Vang, one

of her training partners, shouted from outside the ring.

Another jab from Mika landed, but without as much power. Meghan's body shots were wearing Mika down.

"Meghan, work hard!" shouted Mr. Hodge.

Meghan's balance of attacks with kicks and punches kept Mika from a takedown.

"Thirty seconds!" Mr. Hodge warned. It was the final spar of the night. Mr. Hodge's teen MMA training consisted of drills, instruction, and workouts, and ended with two fighters sparring. Since there were so few female fighters, Meghan sparred often with Mika. Meghan admired her tenacity. Like all the other girls in the dojo, Mika had yet to win against Meghan.

When Mika pushed in for a takedown, Meghan wrapped her arms around Mika's head in a Thai clinch. She couldn't take her down, but she held Mika in place long enough to blast two hard knees into her side. Meghan could hear her gasping for breath. *If you can't breathe,* Meghan thought, *you can't fight back.*

Stronger than Meghan, Mika muscled

Meghan's head downward. Mika brought her knees up for a knee-chin collision that would've resulted in a knockout, except that Meghan unleashed two lightning-fast left hooks into Mika's kidney area first. Mika dropped to one knee. Before Meghan could finish the fight, Mr. Hodge blew the whistle to protect Mika.

Meghan bent down to help Mika up, but Mika waved her away. Mika spit out her mouth guard. Then she spit blood on the mat. Mr. Hodge rushed to her aid.

Meghan climbed out of the ring to accept congratulations from Hector and Jackson. Along with Nong, they were the only four left from the first Missouri MMA teen dojo. In the spring, they'd graduate from high school and the dojo's teen program.

"I said tuck it, and you tucked it." Nong said, fist out to meet Meghan's.

"Be careful, that might be you next," Meghan countered.

"Normally, I wouldn't mind a girl on top of me, but . . ."

Meghan wondered if Nong crushed on her.

Before, she was pretty enough, but now she doubted anyone at school or the dojo wanted her. It didn't matter—the dojo rule was that students didn't date one another. Meghan had her own code: if nobody got close, then nobody could know you, love you, and leave you.

"I'd like to see you two fight," Jackson said.

Nong laughed, then pointed at Meghan. "I doubt I can overcome your secret weapon."

Meghan removed her gloves. "I should know this. What's my secret weapon?" When she took off her protective headgear, her long, light brown hair exploded from underneath the helmet. Mr. Hodge wanted her to cut her hair, but the more hair, the more coverage of the scars on her skull. The scars that weren't hidden, combined with the scowl Jackson had taught her, made Meghan look as tough as any fighter in the dojo.

"Your game face." Nong laughed. Meghan joined in.

After a quick shower, Meghan headed for the door. She grabbed her hoodie on the way out, unlocked her bike, and started the ride to her grandparents' house under a gray sky.

CHAPTER 2

On the way home, Meghan stopped at Starbucks for her normal post-practice Green Tea Frappuccino. While she waited, she turned on her phone and scrolled through the messages.

Once her drink was ready, Meghan went to her table in the back. She sipped the tea as she saw there were texts and Facebook posts from Latasha and Tommy. At one time, they'd all been teammates and best friends, but that was in ninth grade. Before the accident.

The icy drink soothed her, but it didn't stem the ache in her jaw from the most recent spar and the returning pain in other parts of her body. She ignored Latasha's text like she had tried to avoid Tommy the past summer: mostly unsuccessfully.

Meghan looked over photos of Latasha's volleyball game. Latasha looked fierce on the court, although she'd posted that the Lady Raiders lost their first game. They'd fallen far since their conference championship when Meghan, Latasha, and Tommy were ninth graders. Meghan saw two boys walking toward her and put on her best fighter's scowl. They moved past. Meghan smiled at how easily she drove them away.

With her energy restored by calories and caffeine, Meghan biked home in a cold fall rain. Her grandparents' house was dark when she arrived, just past ten. Once inside, Meghan turned on the lights and paused to admire the photos on the wall of her uncle Daniel with his judo, boxing, and MMA honors. There were photos of Meghan with her martial arts honors, as well as dusty trophies and awards in volleyball, basketball, and track. And then there were all the photos of her mother with awards from playing and coaching sports.

Meghan went into the kitchen and saw a note from her grandmother about leftovers in the fridge. She crumpled the note and tossed it in the garbage. Instead, she grabbed an energy drink. Before she left, she examined her grandparents' pillboxes with the meds inside neatly arranged. One box blue, the other pink. Once upstairs, Meghan turned on her light, and opened her bottom dresser drawer. Her pillbox was white and not as organized, but just as full.

Meghan had meds from doctors for everything and anything, real and imagined ailments.

Pills to lose weight and pills to gain muscle. Pills to sleep and pills to wake up. Pills to focus and pills to feel no pain. Meghan had learned how to mix her meds so that nobody noticed a thing.

"We live in a great state," Tommy once said. "Missouri's one of the few where you can doctor shop." Tommy worked the system to stay well stocked. *There's only one better state than Missouri*, Meghan thought, *medicated bliss*. Where there was no noise, no memory, no hard kicks, and no collisions.

CHAPTER 3

"Meghan, we need you."

Meghan stared up at Latasha—most every girl did—but didn't answer.

"I talked to Coach, it's not too late," Latasha said. They stood by Meghan's locker, which she shared with Tommy.

"Great game," a junior girl said to Latasha as she walked past.

"Please, Meghan, we need you," Latasha said softly, even though she stood over six feet.

"I'm done with volleyball. I'm done with playing for a team, you know that," Meghan said. "I fight, for myself." Meghan glanced at the photo of them, along with Tommy, taped to the back of her locker door. Three smiling faces: two white, one black. In between the girls stood the state basketball championship trophy and their coach: Meghan's mom.

"But Meghan, it's been two years and—"

Like many times in the ring, Meghan was saved by the bell. The sounds of lockers shutting echoed through the West High hallways. Finally, Meghan looked at Latasha and whispered, "I'm sorry. I can't. You understand, right?"

Latasha shook her head like she'd been dazed with a quick right jab. "No."

Meghan and Latasha hugged, and Latasha raced off to class. Before Meghan shut the locker, she transferred a wad of bills from her pocket into Tommy's worn denim jacket hanging inside.

⌂ ⌂ ⌂ ⌂ ⌂

After spending most of chemistry class sleeping, Meghan made a quick stop at her locker before lunch. When she walked into the cafeteria, she saw Latasha and her sports friends at a table in the middle. In the back, Tommy sat with her raucous new friends—none of them athletes. Meghan filled up her plate with a salad, forgoing dressing.

"Meghan, here!" Alex, Tommy's boyfriend, shouted. When Meghan arrived at the table, Tommy gave her a hard look. "What's up?"

"Nothing." Meghan sat next to Tommy. Tommy had been point guard, small and smart.

"So, you're actually going to be seen with me in public this year?" Tommy whispered. "I'm not too much of a bad influence?"

"Don't start—it's complicated," Meghan responded. "If I want to be able to fight amateur—" Before she could say another word, laughter exploded from Latasha's table. The third new volleyball coach in three years, a tall black woman in a West High windbreaker, stood eye-to-eye with Latasha. They were all smiles.

Tommy looked hurt watching Latasha. "That used to be us, with your mom." Meghan just stared down at her plate, but Tommy continued. "I wasn't just part of a team, I was part of a family. Your mom was more of a mom to me than my own. So when she—"

Meghan made another fighter's scowl. "Enough! I don't want to talk about it." Meghan covered her scarred face with her long, thin fingers, wishing she could cover it with layers of clothing like she did the rest of her scars. "Money's in your jacket," Meghan whispered.

Under the table, Tommy slipped a small bag of pills into the pocket of Meghan's hoodie.

⸻ ⸻ ⸻ ⸻ ⸻ ⸻

"Meghan, a moment, please," Miss Allison, a school counselor, said. She stood outside Meghan's last-period study hall.

"I'll be late for class," Meghan mumbled through her fog; the Soma had kicked in.

"From what I hear, you'll sleep through it anyway," Miss Allison said. "Follow me."

"Slow down," Meghan requested as she tried to speed-walk behind Allison to her office.

"Sit." Miss Allison pointed at the empty chair. Meghan hated empty chairs.

"Did I do something wrong?" Meghan

asked. She usually stayed out of trouble, partly because when she'd quit all the sports teams, she lost most of her friends and avoided making enemies. Her meds soothed the anger that landed other students in hot water.

"You're sleeping in class again." Miss Allison frowned. She had a good frown, although nothing could match Meghan's mom's pained expression of disappointment.

"You know, it's hard getting back into the swing of the school week with training in the evenings at the dojo."

Another frown. "If you plan to graduate, you'd better get it together."

"I've got it together. Do you?" Meghan's fighter instinct took over: every move has a counter.

Miss Allison's frown fell from disappointment to sadness. "We all miss your mom."

Meghan swallowed hard. Miss Allison had been her mom's best friend.

"If you ever want to talk about it, you—"

"Can I go now?" Meghan snapped. She stood up and turned to leave.

"Of course you can go, Meghan," Miss Allison said. "But can you *let* go? Can you?"

It wasn't a question, but a challenge. Meghan rose to it. She turned back to Miss Allison. "I've got nothing to let go of!"

Miss Allison sighed. "Nothing except all that anger."

Meghan turned, composed herself, and left, waiting for the silence to return.

CHAPTER 4

"So how is school?" Meghan's uncle, Daniel, asked over Sunday brunch at her grandparents' house.

"Okay," Meghan non-answered. Her uncle frowned, followed by a sigh.

Her grandmother pressed the issue. "Meghan, come on, tell your uncle about school."

"Fine." Meghan yawned before giving him a rundown of her first month of senior year. Like dojo practices, her senior year would be structured: tests, college application deadlines, and more tests. Her uncle alternated between nodding in interest and eating his egg-white omelet.

"Are you feeling okay, Megs?" her grandmother asked. "Lately you're either so tired or so energetic. You're like a yo-yo." Meghan's response was another yawn.

"Well, it seems like you'll be busy," Uncle Daniel said. He sounded proud, not worried.

"I wonder where she got that trait from, Daniel?" her grandmother asked. He laughed.

"If you took a vacation, I'd be afraid you'd die," Meghan's grandfather said.

Meghan waited for her uncle to disagree, but he was silent. Even silent, Meghan thought it was nice to have him at the table. Anything was better than that empty chair taunting her.

⬝ ⬝ ⬝ ⬝ ⬝ ⬝

After breakfast, Meghan and her uncle shot baskets in the driveway. While she hadn't played a game in years, she still had her touch. Her uncle was taller and stronger, but Meghan worked hard before losing a game of one-on-one. Like her mom, her uncle never let her win at any sport; they made her compete against their best.

"Go again?" Meghan asked even as pain shot from her still-weak ankles through her body. Before the accident, she'd play all thirty-two minutes of the game. Now, even ten minutes challenged her.

"Sorry, Megs." He glanced at his watch. As far as she knew, the watch was the only thing from her mother that he'd kept. Her mom had gotten it for him after he won his first professional MMA bout. "Busy day, sorry. I'll see you tomorrow." He left, sans hug.

After her uncle left, Meghan went to tell her grandparents she was going out, but both were napping. She kissed her grandmother's forehead, left a note on the kitchen table, grabbed her bike, and headed toward school.

᠁ ᠁ ᠁ ᠁ ᠁

"Let's go, Latasha!" Meghan shouted and clapped.

"Yeah, Latasha!" Tyrell, Latasha's boyfriend, shouted. They'd been together all of high school. Meghan and Tyrell were among only a few dozen people scattered throughout the bleachers for the volleyball game, a far cry from the season when the stands were packed as Meghan's mom led Meghan, Latasha, and Tommy to an undefeated run. From the action on the floor, it looked as if Latasha's senior year might be a winless season. With no one to set for her like Meghan could, or pass like Tommy, Latasha's game and West High's chances of success were flat.

With Meghan and Tyrell leading the cheers, the small crowd made noise, but it wasn't enough as the final minutes wound down. West High lost again. Even from a distance, Meghan saw Latasha holding back tears.

After the game, Meghan biked to Torrey Hill Pizza to join Latasha and Tyrell. When she walked inside, they weren't alone. Her ex, Kevin, and some of his football buddies stood by Latasha's table, and Meghan could tell Latasha wasn't happy about it.

Kevin turned to Meghan. "I was just asking your friend here if she thought the team would show up to actually play a game before the season's over," he said with a smirk.

"Leave her alone," Meghan said, getting in Kevin's face.

His smirk spread into a cocky smile. "It's okay, I guess not everybody can be the star on a winning team," he said.

Latasha jumped in. "Well, we don't all have the advantage you do, with a parent as a coach who plays favorites," Latasha shot back.

"Oh, I guess Meghan's mom didn't play favorites," Kevin said. "You three were all just good enough to start on varsity as freshman," Kevin said. "If you think anybody believes that, you're crazy."

"Maybe I am," Meghan sipped from her water bottle. Her hand shook.

"No wonder I dumped you."

Meghan steadied her hand and then laughed and leaped onto a chair so that she towered over Kevin and his friends. She put her hands in front of her, fingers balled into a fist. "That's right, Kevin, because you're number one!" she said as she lifted the middle finger of each hand.

After Kevin left, Meghan made a quick trip to the bathroom to medicate her anger. When she returned, Latasha was running down the faults of her teammates, but mostly of herself.

"Stop it," Meghan said. "You're the best."

"I used to be," Latasha said.

"*We* used to be," Meghan mumbled.

"Meghan, what's wrong?" Latasha asked. "You're quiet one second, then jumping on chairs the next. When I see you at school, it looks like you just woke up. You okay?"

"Kevin got me worked up, so I just needed a minute to relax, that's all. I'll be fine." Meghan looked at the table to avoid Latasha's gaze. "Latasha, don't worry about me. I don't."

Latasha sighed. "Maybe that's why I think I should."

CHAPTER 5

"I want to spar with Hector at the end of practice tonight," Meghan said. It was an hour before the Monday-night teen class. Only she and Mr. Hodge were at the dojo.

"Meghan, I don't think that's a good idea," Mr. Hodge said.

"You're afraid I'll get hurt?"

Mr. Hodge put his hand on Meghan's shoulder. "That's part of it. It's fine doing the drills with the boys, but sparring isn't a good idea."

"But I'm not going to get better drilling and sparring with the same three or four girls,"

Meghan pressed.

"Maybe, but why not Nong or Shawn, someone closer to your own weight?"

Meghan took her gloves and helmet from her backpack. "Because I can beat both of them, and trust me, you don't want that. It would destroy Nong's confidence."

Mr. Hodge laughed. "Nong's got plenty of confidence."

Meghan shook her head, amazed that Mr. Hodge didn't see through Nong like she did. "No, all that trash talk is just for show. He's really not confident as a fighter."

"Well, he is better in drills than he is in sparring," Mr. Hodge conceded. "Nobody, except maybe you, knows more about MMA than Nong. He's got all the skills."

"It's funny," Meghan said. "Nong has the skills but not the confidence, so he often doesn't win. Jackson lacks the skills, but he usually wins with power and confidence."

"This sport is all about balance," Mr. Hodge said as he helped Meghan with her gloves.

"That's why Hector would be a good match,"

Meghan said. "He's the most balanced fighter in the dojo. If you want me to be a champion, I've got to face better competition."

Mr. Hodge paused and then furrowed his brow. "Okay, but you'll start with Shawn, and only if he's okay with it. We'll do it tomorrow night so he has time to prepare."

"I thought he was taking time off to run cross-country," Meghan asked.

"You know, knowing you, I'm surprised you're not more hooked into the gossip around this place." Mr. Hodge laughed. Meghan said nothing as she put on her practice helmet.

"I'm here to fight, not make friends."

"You seem to be doing a good job on both accounts."

Meghan sighed just before she launched a powerful left hook at Mr. Hodge.

"Is that all you got?!" Mr. Hodge examined the blocker he held in front of him.

Meghan threw an overhand left followed by a right jab and shouted, "I'm here to fight, not make friends!"

"You're sure you're okay with this?" Meghan asked Shawn as they did sit-ups together. "I mean, you won't be upset or anything if I beat you."

Shawn laughed. "It's good that you have dreams, Meghan."

"So why are you not running cross-country?" Meghan knew that Shawn loved MMA, but he also loved playing high school sports. Mr. Hodge let Shawn split his time since Shawn had joined before Mr. Hodge implemented his "no outside sports" rule.

"The thing about cross-country is there's not as much to learn," Shawn explained. "Here, every practice is different because every fight is different. I guess that's why I'll fight you."

"Well, it won't be different for me, because I'll win," Meghan said, smiling.

Shawn laughed again. "Well, either way I lose, so I have no expectations. If I beat you, then I beat a girl, so big deal. If I don't win, then what? But I don't care. I just want to fight."

"Me too."

They were starting to breathe hard as they kept the same pace with each sit-up.

"You're so competitive," Shawn said. "I can't believe you don't play a sport at school. I bet Mr. Hodge would let you. Everybody knows you're his pet."

Meghan scoffed. "I don't think so. More like—what's the opposite of a teacher's pet?"

"OK, more like his protégée." Shawn laughed. "Didn't you ever do school sports?" he asked. Meghan didn't answer as she increased the speed of her sit-ups.

"I bet you did. You would've been a perfect forward in basketball: strong, tall, smart."

Meghan closed her eyes. There she was on the court, finding daylight and driving toward the basket. Tommy had thrown a perfect pass, while Latasha set the screen. Her mom was on the bench directing traffic, yelling, and leading the cheers.

"Volleyball too. Am I right?"

"Is this an interview?" Meghan said between breaths. The smack of someone's fist on the punching bag sounded like the whack of the ball, and Meghan saw herself spiking it.

"You know, you're odd for a teenage girl. Not in a bad way, but just different."

If you only knew, Meghan thought.

"I mean, at my school, every girl your age cares about guys, who's hooking up—all of that."

"All of that's a waste of time." Her stomach burned as sweat drenched her scarred flesh.

"Even how you bike everywhere," Shawn continued. "Man, the second I turned sixteen, I got my license and drove whenever, wherever."

"Shawn, I guess I'll have to punch you in the mouth tomorrow to shut you up."

Shawn laughed. "I'm just curious, that's all. I've known you for almost two years, and I still don't know anything about you. Are you in the Witness Protection Program or what?"

"What."

Shawn laughed again and took a break as Meghan continued doing sit-ups like pistons firing in an engine.

CHAPTER 6

"Any questions?" Mr. Hodge asked the assembled students after explaining his decision to let Meghan begin sparring with the boys. As if on cue, Nong started trash-talking, while Hector said nothing. Meghan knew she'd never spar with Jackson since he was a heavyweight, but Hector was a middleweight.

"Okay, let's see how this goes," Mr. Hodge said. "Meghan and Shawn, let's go."

Mr. Matsuda stood next to Shawn and checked to make sure that all his protective gear was on tight. Mr. Hodge did the same for

Meghan. Meghan heard Mr. Matsuda giving Shawn instructions, but Mr. Hodge said nothing. He just placed his hand on her shoulder and winked.

"Three rounds, two minutes each. Let's work hard!" Mr. Hodge blew the whistle and then moved toward the center of the ring to act as referee.

Shawn and Meghan touched gloves and then assumed a fighting position. Shawn pushed the action as he circled around Meghan, but neither threw a solid strike or tried a takedown.

"Let's go, Meghan!" Meghan heard Mika yell.

"Shawn! Shawn!" The boys started to chant.

Shawn shot in, but Meghan sprawled and held onto Shawn's neck, then moved into an underhook. She tried to throw him but couldn't, even though as a flyweight, he weighed a few pounds less than she did. Shawn pushed out of the underhook and tried for a double leg, but Meghan stuffed him and countered with two kicks that glanced off Shawn's elbow. Shawn fought back and threw the first solid punch, a straight right jab that bounced off Meghan's helmet.

Meghan danced around Shawn before throwing strikes: head hunter hooks followed by body shot kicks. Shawn deflected most of the strikes. As Meghan pressed the action, Shawn backed up until he was against the cage. Meghan clinched and wrapped her arms around the back of Shawn's neck, but as she brought up a heavy knee, Shawn pushed back and took Meghan to the ground. On the ground, Meghan locked in closed guard. Shawn struggled to break the guard and get better position, but Meghan was in firm control even from her back.

With neither fighter gaining an advantage, Mr. Hodge stopped the action and stood them up. More circling followed tentative strikes from Meghan, while Shawn kept trying for a takedown.

"Thirty seconds!" Mr. Matsuda shouted.

Meghan faked a roundhouse kick to Shawn's side, then caught him off guard with a right jab, an overhand left, and an uppercut. The whistle blew before Meghan could inflict more damage.

When Mr. Hodge blew the whistle to start round two, Shawn came out swinging. Using his small reach advantage, Shawn punched, stepped back, and set up another strike. Meghan defended with front kicks, but they didn't slow Shawn down. Then, when Shawn missed a left hook, Meghan locked him in the clinch and pulled his head down while lifting her knee up. The crack of her knee against his jaw was followed by the thud of Shawn's back hitting the mat.

On the mount, Meghan dropped hammer fists. Using a butterfly guard, Shawn hooked Meghan's thighs with his ankles, underhooked her arm, pushed up, and elevated Meghan from her mount. As Meghan tried to balance with her right arm, Shawn snatched it between his legs and rolled through. Before Meghan could escape the arm bar, Mr. Hodge blew the whistle to end the fight.

Shawn released the hold, stood, and helped Meghan to her feet. She managed not to wince as he pulled her up by her right arm. They took out their mouth guards. "Good fight," Meghan said.

"I got lucky," Shawn said as they touched gloves.

"No, you got skills, but I got something too."

"What's that?"

As she watched Shawn's right hand being raised, she whispered, "Motivation."

⸫ ⸫ ⸫ ⸫ ⸫ ⸫

In her usual Starbucks corner spot, Meghan scrolled through messages and posts in between sips of her Green Tea Frappuccino. She felt her arm starting to throb. Perhaps she could have worked her way out of the hold, perhaps not, but Mr. Hodge should have given her a chance. She worried that she wouldn't get another shot against the boys. She knew she could beat Shawn if given one more opportunity. She'd just need to avoid a takedown, find a better balance.

The green tea perked her up but seemed to make her arm hurt more. She called Tommy.

"Hey, I'm sorry about that thing at school the other day."

"Me too," Tommy said. "Maybe because it's

volleyball season, I'm thinking about—"

"Don't." Meghan threw the word like a perfect kick.

Tommy paused. "I wonder how things would be different for all of us," she said.

Meghan sensed the sadness in her voice and changed the subject. "What are you doing tonight?"

"Party," Tommy said.

"Something new and different for you," Meghan quipped. She rubbed her sore right arm with her left hand. "Where?"

Tommy laughed. "Meghan, don't you know me? The party is wherever I am."

CHAPTER 7

"So, maybe next week, you and I can go?" Meghan asked Nong. They were in the far corner of the dojo, doing sit-ups to warm up.

"You don't want any of the Ninja Warrior," Nong said and laughed. "Besides, don't you think you should beat Shawn first before talking trash about me?"

"We're going again tonight," Meghan answered as she hit the fifty sit-up mark.

"So what's your plan?" Nong asked.

"Why? Are you his spy?"

Nong laughed. "I want you to win. I mean,

I like Shawn and all, but you, me, Hector, and Jackson have been training together from the start. We're like family."

"Family," Meghan mumbled, embarrassed.

"Something like that," Nong said, also sounding embarrassed.

"Well, then it'll be such a shame to beat you up, big brother," Meghan said.

"No, I'm the little brother," Nong said. "The Ninja Warrior is an underdog wonder."

Meghan just laughed. She thought Nong's Ninja Warrior trash talk was funny, although Mr. Hodge didn't like it. Meghan thought Nong would've figured that out by now.

"You've fought Shawn. How do you beat him?" Meghan asked.

As always, Nong kind of rambled, comparing his spars against Shawn with great MMA fights of the past, but ended with a big smile. "Shawn's tough to beat, but he's inexperienced. So when he makes a mistake, you take advantage, Ninja Warrior style."

After listening to Nong, Meghan found Hector and Jackson throwing strikes against the heavy bag. Jackson threw thunder, strong and loud; Hector threw lightning-fast punches. She asked them the same question.

"Shawn is streaky," Jackson said. "He's hot or cold. He doesn't have a balanced game."

"He's on-again and off-again at the dojo, so he doesn't have our mental toughness," Hector said. "In the cage, he lays back until he gets a chance and then comes out swinging."

"Same thing on the ground," Jackson said. They were still throwing punches as they spoke. Mr. Hodge never wanted to see anyone standing still. In the dojo, you moved—or moved out. "Once he gets somebody down, he'll do nothing and then explode. You need to catch him between."

"When he's vulnerable," Hector said. "You get him when he thinks he's in control."

"Thanks guys," Meghan said. She wanted to touch gloves to show her respect, but Hector and Jackson never stopped drilling—Mr. Hodge would be proud. Meghan was ready to make him prouder. She'd fight a smarter fight so he wouldn't need to protect her again.

"Let's do the same as last time," Mr. Hodge said. "Three rounds of two minutes."

Shawn and Meghan touched gloves and returned to their corners. Before the whistle blew, Meghan noticed that Jackson, Nong, and Hector stood apart from the other students. They'd positioned themselves near Meghan's corner. They cheered when she landed the first strike: a solid body shot kick to Shawn's side.

Just as before, Shawn alternated quick strikes with takedown attempts, and Meghan defended with sprawls, clinches, and kicks. After each of his failed attempts, Shawn retreated toward the ropes, which allowed Meghan to press the action. She continued with kicks, knees, and punches to the body. If she couldn't knock him out, she'd knock the wind out of him.

The round ended with neither fighter in control. Nong, Hector, and Jackson came up to the ring during the break. "I'd give that round to him, but keep up with those body shots," Nong said. "It makes it harder for him to breathe."

Hector nodded. "He can't explode if his tank is empty," he added.

Jackson clapped with the others as the whistle blew.

Meghan started the round with another roundhouse to the body, but Shawn held onto her left leg. He tripped her to score the takedown. Meghan landed with good position, not allowing Shawn to mount. He struggled to maintain even side control, which allowed Meghan to sweep from underneath and regain her feet. As Shawn tried to stand, Meghan clinched his neck.

"Guillotine!" Nong shouted, but Shawn was too strong, and Meghan couldn't get her hands locked. Shawn got to his feet and waited for Meghan to bring the fight to him.

"Let's work hard, Shawn!" Mr. Hodge said. Shawn responded by rushing toward Meghan, but she was ready. She threw two hard left hooks to the body followed by a roundhouse kick to the ribs. Meghan could hear Shawn gasping for breath. She threw a lazy front kick, and Shawn took her down again with another single leg. But on the way down, she controlled his body.

When Shawn tried a strike from the mount, Meghan grabbed his right wrist and pulled. She unlocked her feet and scooted out. Before Shawn could pass guard, Meghan sat up. She quickly wrapped her right arm around Shawn's exposed right shoulder and locked it on her left wrist.

With Shawn's arm firmly in her control, Meghan rolled back, put her right foot on Shawn's left hip, and threw her left leg high over his back to lock him in position, completing the Kimura. The submission hold put her in total control. Shawn tapped in an instant. Mr. Hodge blew the whistle, and Meghan heard applause surround her just like she used to hear on the hardwood courts in practice. *You're not just an athlete*, Meghan recalled her mom telling her over and over. *You're a champion*. When Mr. Hodge raised her hand, she pointed one finger toward heaven.

≡ ≡ ≡ ≡ ≡

Meghan described every second of the fight to Latasha as they sat in her normal spot at Starbucks. With some pills and a Frap coursing through her, Meghan rambled until Latasha reached across the table and clasped Meghan's shaking left hand. "What are you doing?" Meghan asked, shaking her hand free.

"I can tell something's going on," Latasha whispered. "You were fine ten minutes ago. You're totally wired now."

"Nothing's going on. I'm just excited about getting a W."

"Look, I've played sports my entire life. I know a problem when I see it."

"What problem?" Meghan laughed, Latasha didn't.

"You're a pill head," Latasha whispered. "I know you'll deny it, because that's what addicts do."

Meghan wasn't laughing anymore. "I'm not a pill head," she whispered back. "I don't have a problem, and it's none of your business."

"We said we'd watch out for each other, so I'm keeping my part of that deal."

"I don't need you to do that." Meghan felt like hurling the cup against the wall. She stood up to leave, but Latasha grabbed her wrist.

"Did you ever see a hamster in a cage?" Latasha said.

Meghan didn't answer. She used all of her energy to keep from exploding at Latasha.

"That's you. You're like a hamster on one of those wheels. You keep running and running in place, but listen, Meghan, you're getting nowhere."

"You don't know what you're talking about!" Meghan hissed and started for the door.

Latasha grabbed her arm. "You have to take a pill to go to sleep and then one to wake up. You take a pill to feel good, and when that wears off, you take another. You take one to stop the pain, but it just keeps coming back."

"MMA is a hard sport. I get hurt more in one day than you do in a season."

Latasha loosened her grip on Meghan's arm but leaned in closer. "That's not the pain I'm talking about, and you know it."

Meghan glared at Latasha with a fighter's scowl but said nothing. She turned and walked away. Latasha followed behind her, yelling, "You gotta get off the wheel, Meghan."

CHAPTER 8

"Meghan, wake up!" Her grandmother's voice sounded concerned.

Meghan slowly opened her eyes to see her extended family sitting around the table at her grandparents' house. She'd fallen asleep in the middle of the Thanksgiving meal.

"Are you okay?" her grandmother asked.

"Just tired," Meghan answered.

"Maybe you should get some sleep every now and then," her uncle said.

"Maybe she shouldn't spend so much time at the dojo," her grandmother countered.

"Maybe I'm tired of this bickering," Meghan said, which silenced the room. She stared at her uncle. He looked at her with suspicion like Miss Allison did at school.

Meghan's aunt Judy broke the silence. "Megs, can you join us to go shopping Saturday evening?"

"Thanks, but I'm busy. I'm going over to Shawn's to watch a UFC pay-per-view."

"Oh, goodness, they even fight on Thanksgiving weekend. Honestly, Daniel, I don't know how you got hooked up with this, and now to have your niece fighting too?"

"I fight for me, not for him," Meghan said, which wasn't entirely true. She wanted to please her uncle. She also had no choice of other sports. She'd been an athlete all her life, but the accident robbed her of the mobility and speed crucial to the team sports she used to do. She couldn't run, jump, or drive to the basket. She could only stand and fight.

"Can we talk about something else?" Meghan's grandmother asked. She led the conversation in a different direction, while

Meghan fought the urge to drift off to sleep.

"I'll be right back." Meghan excused herself from the table, grabbed her purse, and went into the bathroom. Some girls at the dojo purged to make weight. *But why stick fingers down your throat*, she thought, *when you could just swallow a pill?*

␣ ␣ ␣ ␣ ␣ ␣

"Honey, could we speak with you for a minute?" Meghan's grandfather said when she returned. Her grandparents stood in the kitchen, away from the rest of the family.

Meghan nodded and rested against the countertop. "We know you've been working very hard trying to juggle school, helping out around the house, and fighting," her grandmother said.

Meghan braced herself for the blow.

"You need a vacation from all of this," her grandmother continued.

"A vacation?"

"We know you have some heavy training coming up for your first amateur fight. But first, we all think you need to clear your head, rest your body, and reset your focus," her grandmother said.

"Where are we going?" she asked.

"We're not," her grandmother said. "We're sending you and your uncle to Hawaii for your winter break. I know it will be tough being in the Hawaiian sun rather than the cold, damp Missouri December." Her grandparents laughed.

"Is something wrong?" her grandfather asked.

"Can I bring one of my friends with me instead of Uncle Daniel?" Meghan asked.

"No, this was actually his idea. He's worried about you too," her grandfather said. Her grandparents' eyes glanced away, avoiding hers.

"But I bet Latasha would—" Meghan started.

"Won't she have a holiday tournament like you used to have?" her grandfather asked.

"How about Tommy?" Meghan asked. Her grandparents frowned in unison.

After a pause, her grandmother spoke. "We think it's best that you not spend time with Tommy."

"Why?" Meghan decided to press them. See what they actually knew.

More eyes darting back and forth. "She's a bad influence," her grandfather offered.

"You don't get to pick my friends!" Meghan said more loudly.

"You're right," her grandfather said. "You're only months away from being an adult. But I guess we had hoped you'd make better choices."

"You don't know anything about Tommy," Meghan countered.

"We know enough," her grandfather said.

"How? From whom?" Meghan shouted. Her grandparents didn't answer. Meghan fumed as it came to her. They didn't know about Tommy's pill connections, but somebody else did. And she had talked.

॰   ॰ ॰ ॰ ॰ ॰ ॰

"How dare you!" Meghan shouted into the phone, sitting on her bed with her door closed.

"Happy Thanksgiving to you too," Latasha replied.

"What are you doing talking with my

grandparents about Tommy?" Meghan asked.

"Drastic times call for drastic measures," Latasha said. "I could tell you weren't listening to me, so I thought maybe you'd listen to family. Even though I thought that's what we were."

"Stay out of this."

"You're still like family to me, no matter what," Latasha said. "Tell me what I can do to help."

"Like I said, stay out of my business," Meghan snapped. "Tommy's my friend."

"She used to be our friend," Latasha said. "Now, to her, you're just income."

In one swift motion, Meghan hung up the phone and opened her pillbox. She swallowed four Somas and waited for the dreamy state to kick in. With the pills, there was no before, no after, no pain; there was here, now, and joyful nothingness. The Somas were like a KO punch she welcomed every night.

CHAPTER 9

"Meghan, come here," Mr. Matsuda called out as Meghan walked into the dojo. She jogged over to where Mr. Matsuda stood. Next to him was a girl who reminded Meghan of Latasha— just as tall and athletic-looking.

"Meghan, this is Josie Roberts. She's a black belt in jiu-jitsu, thanks to me." The girl bowed to Mr. Matsuda, and they laughed. "Nice to meet you," Meghan said.

"She's been training over at the MMA Academy and—"

"I'd love to train here with Mr. Matsuda, but

it's too far from my house," Josie said.

"She's only trained in MMA for about a year, but she has a solid background," Mr. Matsuda continued. "But she's got the same problem you have. No real competition, so we thought—"

"Yes!" Meghan shouted. Josie laughed.

"So she'll join us for drills tonight, and then you two will spar at the end of the night, OK?"

"I'm ready to rumble," Josie replied and picked up her gym bag. "You ready to bring it?"

Meghan stared her down, but Josie kept smiling. Why wasn't she scared? With Meghan's fearsome scowl and scarred face—Josie wouldn't know the scars didn't come from fighting—Josie should be shaking. Meghan wondered if Josie had a secret weapon too.

⌐ ⌐ ⌐ ⌐ ⌐

"So, what do you think?" Meghan asked Jackson as they drilled together.

Jackson threw a hard right against the blocker, which knocked Meghan back an inch.

"I think it's a great idea," Jackson said. "I hope we all get a chance to do that."

"Do what?" Hector said as he walked over. Nong was a step behind with the blocker.

Meghan explained how she'd get to spar with Josie, to practice fighting a better-matched and less familiar opponent. Like Jackson, Hector seemed interested in doing the same, though he hardly showed it. Nong talked a lot without really saying anything. A normal night at the dojo.

"Hey, I'm going to Hawaii for Christmas break since the dojo is closed," Meghan said.

"Sweet," Nong said. "Maybe you'll run into BJ Penn."

"Who?" Meghan asked.

"He was the second fighter in UFC history to win titles in two different weight classes," Nong said.

"Who was first?" Hector asked.

"UFC Hall of Famer Randy Couture," Nong said. "You know who is next to do that?"

"Jon Jones?" Jackson offered up the name of his MMA hero.

"Nong 'The Ninja Warrior' Vang, that's who!" Nong shouted, then threw an air kick.

Meghan laughed, while Hector and Jackson just shook their heads in some strange combination of amusement and disgust. "Well, first, you've gotta win in amateur, Ninja Warrior."

As they drilled, they talked about their first amateur fights, which would happen soon after their eighteenth birthdays. Meghan's fight would be right after they graduated from high school, while the others would fight before.

The topic turned to their plans for after high school. Nong and Hector wanted to dedicate themselves full-time to training, while Jackson's goal was to join the Army Special Forces.

"What about you, Meghan?" Jackson asked. Meghan handed Jackson the blocker. She answered only with a shrug before she started throwing hard kicks and harder punches.

ɛ ɛ ɛ ɛ ɛ

Mr. Hodge stood in the middle of the ring. Although Josie was around the same weight as Meghan, Josie had a slight reach advantage. Long arms, Meghan knew, could easily be snatched into a submission. If she could Kimura someone stronger than her, like Shawn, then Josie should be easy pickings.

"Three rounds of two minutes," Mr. Hodge said. "Protect yourself at all times."

Meghan extended her glove, and Josie touched. They went to their corners to await the whistle. Everybody in the dojo sat on the mat and waited. Meghan sensed the anticipation in everyone but herself. She hadn't mentally prepared for a hard spar.

At the whistle, Meghan faked a kick and started to circle. She knew that Josie could dominate on strikes with her reach advantage, but if she had a jiu-jitsu background, she'd also be tough on the mat. Like with Shawn, the key was to cut her wind and force a mistake.

Josie threw a hard right, but her left was weak and she didn't try to throw any kicks. Meghan tried kicks to the body and legs, but Josie defended them well. Over and over, Josie tried to get Meghan to the mat. Meghan blocked every shot. With the round winding down, Josie got Meghan's left leg elevated, but Meghan stayed balanced and wouldn't go down. As the first round ended, neither fighter had scored a takedown or a solid strike, although Josie had pushed the action more.

"You lost that round," Mr. Hodge said to Megan during the break. "Are you going to work hard or not?"

Meghan banged her gloves together and raced to the middle of the ring when the whistle blew. When Josie tried an overhand left, Meghan responded with a jab to the body and followed up with knees. Then she took Josie over with a sweeping hip throw. On the ground, Meghan tried to get position, but Josie's long arms fought her off. Even though Meghan had the mount, Josie controlled with a closed guard. When Meghan felt Josie's leg creep up her back into rubber guard to set up a submission, Meghan passed guard and regained her feet.

Josie quickly stood, and they began exchanging strikes. Soon Mr. Hodge blew the whistle to end the round.

"What's your plan?" Mr. Hodge asked Meghan between rounds. Meghan took out her mouthpiece and swallowed some water. Mr. Hodge lowered his voice and looked her in the eyes. "If she's stronger than you, then use your quickness. Get in, fire some body shots, and stay away from takedowns." Meghan nodded. "You have the skills, so use them!"

Meghan put in her mouthpiece and waited for the whistle. In the opposite corner, Mr. Matsuda was talking with Josie. Was he encouraging her or telling her Meghan's flaws?

To start the third round, Meghan exploded with a series of kicks to Josie's legs, but Josie responded with a hard right. Another hard right to the side of the head buckled Meghan's knees for a second. That was all it took. Josie swarmed Meghan and showered her with wild strikes: jabs, hooks, knees, and kicks. They came from every angle, too many defend against. It was happening both too fast to react and in slow motion. Just like the accident.

Josie grabbed a clinch and executed a textbook judo throw. She got full mount position as Meghan fought to get half guard. Meghan stopped a hard right coming toward her jaw, but she couldn't stop the left elbow strike that split her open just above the right eye.

"That's it!" Mr. Hodge shouted and waved his hands in the air. Before he raised Josie's hand, he bent down to Meghan. Somebody threw a towel into the ring, and he handed it to her.

Meghan wiped the blood and spit from her mouthpiece. "You okay?" Mr. Hodge asked.

"I'm good," Meghan answered and then looked up at Josie. "But she's better, tonight."

"She was faster than you. I didn't think that would be the case," Mr. Hodge said. "Or maybe you were just moving in slow motion so everybody could watch you fight?"

Meghan sat up, pressed the towel against her bloody forehead, and moved from Mr. Hodge toward Josie. She took the towel away and saw the red stain in the middle of the white fabric. She tasted the blood that had dripped into her mouth. *So that's what defeat tastes like*, she thought. She looked up at Josie and saw the smile on her face. Meghan smiled along with her.

"Enjoy it while you can," Meghan said. "Because next time will be different."

Josie took out her mouthpiece. "What makes you think so?"

Meghan couldn't tell her the truth. The meds had begun diluting her fighting skills—she could tell she wasn't thinking as fast on her feet. In a few weeks, she'd go to Hawaii with her uncle, get clean, get her mind right, and get her fight game back. It wasn't even the sun, the ocean, or the food that she was looking forward to. It was the chance to get a few thousand miles away from her life and finally get off the wheel.

"I'll win," Meghan said, trying to hide her smile, "because I've got nothing left to lose."

CHAPTER 10

"I'm sorry." Meghan stood in front of Latasha's locker on the first day of school after winter break with a box of macadamia nuts in front of her. Her tan was already fading, along with the craving for pills. "You were only trying to help."

Latasha nodded. "And did I?" she asked as she took the box.

"I think so. I went my entire vacation without, you know," Meghan said. "And I stopped in the office this morning and I'm getting my locker changed, so that's a small step."

"I'm glad to hear that," Latasha said. "You

want to take a bigger step?"

"What?"

"Join the basketball team again. We need you, bad," Latasha said and laughed. "We lost every game of the holiday tournament. Nobody but me shot over fifty percent. It's horrible."

"I can't. I need to focus on my fighting," Meghan said. "I have my first fight coming up right after we graduate, and I want you to be there."

"Will I finally get to meet all of your dojo friends?" Latasha asked.

Meghan shrugged but said nothing. She kept her balance—and her secrets—by not mixing friends.

"Seriously, think about coming back. I know you're hurt, but I bet you could still shoot and rebound." Meghan's mom had coached them for hours on rebound positioning. It was one of the only skills Meghan still had on the court after her injuries from the accident.

"Meghan!" Latasha shouted. "You zoned out. You're sure you're clean?"

Meghan nodded, smiled, and then headed off toward the office. She took a path so she wouldn't pass by her old locker, by Tommy, or by the little pills of Tommy's that offered big temptation. She would see Miss Allison as well and let her view Meghan in an alert, non-Soma state.

* * * * *

Meghan avoided the cafeteria and ignored Tommy's texts throughout the morning, but she knew she had to confront her face-to-face at some point. They arranged to meet during lunch at a city park near school. Meghan cleaned the snow off the swings as she waited for Tommy.

"What's the story?" Tommy asked when she arrived. Meghan was already on the swings.

Meghan waited until Tommy sat in the swing next to her. "I need to tell you something."

"I thought you already did by changing lockers. That's a pretty clear message," Tommy said.

"I didn't clear out everything. I left that picture of the three of us."

"Four of us." She paused. "Your mom really did mean a lot to me." Tommy started to swing. Meghan joined. "What did I do to you, Meghan?"

"It's just that I need to change things in my life," Meghan said slowly, unsure of what to say and how to say it. Finally she just said it. "I don't think I can be friends with you anymore."

"Did your uncle tell you this on your big vacation in the sun, while I was stuck over here, freezing my butt off in Missouri? Or did you come to this realization elsewhere?"

Meghan didn't tell her the truth; she'd seen very little of the beach. Most of it was spent fighting off the effects of self-detox. She kicked her legs to swing higher. "No, this is my decision."

"So what did I do to you?" Tommy asked again.

"I'm tired. I'm tired of needing pills to wake up, go to sleep, make me feel better or not feel anything. If we stay friends, share the same locker, it's just too tempting. I'm not saying we can't be friends ever again, but—"

"We said that we'd—all three of us—we'd be friends forever. Remember?"

"That was a long time ago. A lot has changed," Meghan said softly.

Tommy lit up a cigarette. "We said we'd win

state titles every year, and then we'd get NCAA scholarships. And we'd tell the recruiters that we wanted to stay together."

"I have to move forward, Tommy. I have to let go of that."

Tommy blew a smoke ring that mixed with her frosty breath. "Fine. I don't need you." She got up off the swing. "But you need me, and you know it."

Meghan didn't respond. Part of her wanted to leap off the swing at the highest point and land hard on the ground, maybe shattering her ankles again. It would be an excuse to get stronger pain pills from a doctor—how she'd gotten hooked in the first place. But instead she kicked to swing even faster and higher as she watched Tommy walk away.

⬚ ⬚ ⬚ ⬚ ⬚ ⬚

"I wanted to let you know, I'm feeling better," Meghan told Miss Allison.

"I'm glad to hear that." Miss Allison motioned for Meghan to sit, but she stayed standing.

"Good enough to play tennis come spring?"

Miss Allison was the girls' tennis coach.

"I can't, you know, because of . . . And I'm still fighting, so no, I can't."

"That's a shame. You had all the makings of a champion."

Meghan laughed. "I seem to recall losing more than I won my freshman year."

"No—it's like your mother used to say." Miss Allison's words were garbled. Meghan wondered if she was holding back tears. "You're not just an athlete, you're a champion."

"What do you mean?" Meghan had never looked deeper into this riddle.

"An athlete is someone who competes in sports, but a champion is—"

Meghan jumped in. "Good enough to win?"

"No, that's a winner," Miss Allison said. "To your mom, to me, probably to your uncle too, being a champion isn't just about winning, but living your life the right way. An athlete has the tools to do well in sports, but a champion has the tools to succeed both on and off the court."

CHAPTER 11

"Nong, how about it?" Meghan asked.

Nong just shook his head like he was tired of saying no to Meghan. She'd asked Nong to spar every night since the start of the year, and the answer was always the same.

Last weekend, they'd piled into the dojo van—one of the few vehicles she'd ride in—with Hector, Jackson, and Mr. Hodge to go to an MMA card, and they stood together in the cage before the show. It made her upcoming fight seem real. Then Mr. Hodge had announced they'd be sparring soon with fighters from the

MMA Academy, another local dojo. Meghan hadn't fought pill-free in forever, and she'd started to wonder if she could stand the pain.

"Look, don't you think it would help you prepare to fight someone like me?" she pressed Nong.

"How is fighting a girl going—"

"I'm not a girl, I'm a fighter. Get in the ring with me and I'll show you."

Nong shook his head. Meghan didn't know if it was in disbelief or anger, but before she could ask she heard a deep male voice. "I'll do it."

Meghan turned around. Eric Shaw stood behind her. He was also seventeen and fought at light heavyweight. He weighed fifty pounds more than Meghan and was taller and stronger, but way less experienced. The last time he was in the spar with Hector, a middleweight, Eric had tapped.

"Really?" Meghan didn't know Eric well, other than that he wasn't as skilled as she was.

"Look, the only way I'm going to get better is to fight," Eric said. "So, no excuses, let's go full out. I'll ask Mr. Hodge if it's okay."

"Of course it's okay."

"Well, he might not think it's a fair fight."

Meghan laughed. "It won't be a fair fight, Eric. It will be a short one."

※ ※ ※ ※ ※

"Okay, let's work hard for three rounds of two minutes," Mr. Hodge said to Meghan and Eric as they stood across from each other. They touched gloves and returned to their corners until Mr. Hodge blew the whistle. As always, every eye in the dojo was trained on the ring.

Eric didn't waste any time as he came right at Meghan with short jabs and shot for a takedown, but Meghan sprawled and then scampered to the other side of the ring. Eric followed, threw more jabs, and went for another takedown, but Meghan got a knee up. It cracked hard against Eric's helmet. Meghan tried for a Thai clinch, but Eric easily escaped. As Eric circled, Meghan threw front kicks more for defense than as strikes. After taking the knee, Eric seemed more apprehensive about a takedown and threw short jabs. Although he had the reach, he didn't have the timing, and his punches didn't connect with power. Meghan slipped a left hook and tried a takedown, but she couldn't budge Eric from his base. Meghan felt Eric underhook her arms, but she blocked his takedown. It was a stand-up stalemate.

"Let's work hard, Eric! You too, Meghan!" Mr. Hodge yelled. Eric kept his chin tucked and head down as he barreled toward Meghan. Her strikes did little damage as Eric bullied her against the ropes. Locked in a clinch, Meghan and Eric exchanged short rights and lefts. They dirty boxed against the ropes until Mr. Hodge blew the whistle to end the round.

"Are you okay?" Mr. Hodge asked Meghan during the break. "Do you want to quit?"

Meghan pounded her gloves together and shook her head no. She'd work through the pain the best way a fighter can: end the fight as soon as possible. When the whistle blew for round two, Meghan kept her distance and defended against Eric's punches and kicks. They circled for a while, neither throwing strikes, looking more like helmeted dancers than fighters. Mr. Hodge clapped his hands together, encouraging them to engage. "Let's work hard, people, work hard!"

Meghan threw a roundhouse kick that landed hard on Eric's hip and made him wince, but a repeat kick allowed Eric to grab Meghan's right leg. He followed through by tripping her left leg, and they crashed hard to the mat with Eric on top. As they hit the floor, Eric's shoulder jammed hard against Meghan's jaw. Eric threw short elbows from the mount while Meghan tried to sweep, but even with her legs in near perfect position on Eric's shin and knee, she couldn't move his weight. She worked from half guard back to closed guard quickly to limit Eric's strikes. Once she locked it in, Eric could muster little offense. Mr. Hodge stood the fighters up.

Back on her feet, Meghan attempted a double leg. Instead of sprawling, Eric took Meghan down with a double underhook. As they tumbled to the mat, Meghan got free but hung onto Eric's right arm. On the ground, Meghan maneuvered her legs across Eric's chest, with his right arm between her thighs and his left elbow tucked against her hip. Meghan pulled Eric's forearm across her chest to set up the arm bar submission. She leaned back and lifted her hips, which put pressure on Eric's arm. He tried to stand, pull his arm free, and roll away, but Meghan's grip was tight and her control total. Eric tapped just as Mr. Hodge whistled the fight to an end.

"That was just about perfect," Mr. Hodge whispered to Meghan. Meghan took a deep breath as Mr. Hodge raised her hand. She held it in the air for a long, long time. Her jaw ached and her ankles throbbed, but to earn the W, the pain was well worth it.

⸢ ⸢ ⸢ ⸢ ⸢ ⸢

When Meghan biked home in the cold, she felt the pain set in all over her body. She'd absorbed more blows than she realized, but mostly her jaw hurt. As she waited for her drink at Starbucks, she went into the restroom and looked at her face in the mirror. A new deep bruise on her cheek joined old scars from the accident.

The cold beverage felt like it drove a spike into her forehead as it moved down her throat. She took only one sip before she tossed it in the trash and continued her journey home. A hot shower did nothing to ease the pain, nor did four aspirin. Meghan couldn't sleep as she used one hand to gently rub her sore jaw and the other to scroll through messages and posts on her phone.

Even though her grandparents kept the temperature in the house cool, Meghan started to sweat. Another shower didn't help to stop the sweat or the pain. Only one thing would do that.

After the shower she looked at herself in mirror. Her body was muscled and taut from years of training, but scarred from a few seconds of tragedy. The girls at the dojo never said anything about the scars she usually kept hidden. Even Latasha and Tommy hadn't seen these secret scars.

She picked up her phone, and her thumb traced the outside of the keypad. All of her pain could be over if she hit Tommy's number. But she thought about the numbers before Tommy's:

her grandparents, her uncle, and Latasha. She'd be letting them all down. She turned off her phone and went downstairs, feeling like she'd just gotten another W.

But while Meghan sat at the kitchen table with an ice bag on her jaw, pain overwhelmed pride, and she realized she didn't need Tommy's help. She put the ice bag away and walked over to the pink pillbox on the counter. Her grandma's memory wasn't that good anyway; she'd think she just forgot to put out the white pain pill, now in Meghan's hand.

CHAPTER 12

"Meghan, are you ready?" Mr. Matsuda asked. They stood outside of the locker room at the MMA Academy. Meghan wouldn't change in a locker room with strangers, so she came dressed to fight. She nodded her head and threw hard strikes into the blocker. It didn't hurt at all.

"You're on last," Mr. Matsuda said. "And don't let being in the cage throw you. Same skills as in the ring, just a different setting."

Meghan nodded again and threw a wicked high kick. It was easy for Mr. Matsuda to say *don't let it get to you*—he wasn't going into the cage. He didn't need to save the day for Mr. Hodge. Of the three Missouri MMA students who had sparred with MMA Academy fighters, only Hector had won. Nong had tapped, and Jackson lost by decision. This fight wasn't for her, but for the dojo.

"Since she's shorter than you, you have the reach advantage," Mr. Matsuda said. "Get your strikes in early and then take her down. Get her off balance while you stay solid, and you win. Simple."

Meghan nodded for the third time. One for each round, except it wasn't going to last three rounds like Jackson's fight. She wanted to end it right away.

"It's time," Mr. Matsuda said. He patted Meghan on the shoulder. As he walked away, Meghan moved toward where she'd set her sweatshirt and took out some pills. She went to the drinking fountain and promised herself this was the last time, the very last time. Meghan swallowed the pills, put in her mouthpiece, and headed slowly to the cage.

⬜ ⬜ ⬜ ⬜ ⬜ ⬜

Mr. Hodge stood in the middle of the cage as referee. Meghan stared at him: would he stop the fight to protect Meghan from getting hurt like he had when she fought Josie? Or would he let her fight back?

The fighter from the MMA Academy came into the cage, head down. She and Meghan had weighed in just a few pounds apart, but Amy Lee was at least three inches shorter, squat, and probably stronger. Although Meghan wasn't fighting Josie again—Meghan knew the purpose of the spar was to fight somebody new—it felt like a re-match. This time the result would be different.

Mr. Hodge gave the instructions to both fighters but seemed to be looking only at Meghan when he talked about protecting yourself and tapping out before getting injured. Meghan listened and stared at the mat. No doubt Amy was staring up at her.

When the whistle blew, the fighters touched gloves and assumed their stances. Meghan circled and waited. Amy started with her right jab, but Meghan slipped it and responded with an inside leg kick. Every time Amy tried to shoot,

Meghan sprawled to avoid the takedown. Amy pressed the action, while Meghan reacted and waited for an opportunity.

When Amy's takedown attempt using a double underhook landed them against the cold chain-link cage, Meghan opened up her offense. With Amy's hands locked under Meghan's arms, Amy couldn't defend herself. Meghan landed strikes against Amy's helmet and buried knees in her gut. Amy dropped the underhook, allowing Meghan to change levels, scoop Amy's left leg, trip her right, and take her down right at the "thirty seconds" call. On the ground, Meghan got side control, but Amy powered up and out as the round ended.

"Good round," Mr. Matsuda said as Meghan tried to catch her breath. "Not sure if he'll give it to you, but good round." Mr. Matsuda gave Meghan some tips for getting a takedown. Meghan nodded but knew words didn't matter at this point. She ran on adrenaline, athletic instinct from years of training, and black-market amphetamines.

The fighters touched gloves to start the second round. It quickly mirrored the first: Amy trying to use her strength to take Meghan down, and Meghan defending with strikes. As Amy stepped in to throw a left hook, Meghan dropped down, snatched Amy's thick legs, and pushed her against the cage, but couldn't take her down. Against the cage, Amy seemed to freeze while Meghan worked with punches to the head, knees to the body, and kicks to Amy's legs. As Amy pushed back to create distance, Meghan threw a hard knee that stunned Amy. Meghan faked another knee, which got Amy's hands down, and Meghan hit a lightning-fast combination that rocked Amy and pitched her head forward. Her head then absorbed the blow of a high kick.

"Thirty seconds!"

The head kick buckled Amy's knees. Meghan pounced with a right jab, an overhead left, and an uppercut that landed hard on Amy's chin as the round ended.

"You've got her scared, but she's got to take you down in order to win," Mr. Matsuda said before the last round. "She's getting tired and frustrated. She'll make a mistake, and you'll tap her out."

Meghan pounded her gloves as the whistle blew. After touching gloves, Amy rushed forward. She threw short, powerful right jabs that Meghan mostly deflected; the strikes lacked the snap of earlier in the fight. When Amy tried a takedown, Meghan sprawled and locked her hands deep around Amy's neck. Meghan fired a hard uppercut to the chin. Amy pushed back and escaped Meghan's clinch. But every move Amy tried, Meghan answered. In desperation, Amy started throwing overhand lefts that barely grazed Meghan's helmet. When Amy tried a high kick, Meghan blocked it and followed with a sweeping hip throw.

"Thirty seconds."

On the ground, when Amy tried to push back to get distance, Meghan snatched her right arm, just as she had done with Eric. She quickly unlocked her legs to move to Amy's side as the seconds ticked down. But the time ran out before she could lock in the arm bar submission.

Meghan soaked in the applause from members of her dojo as she stood next to Mr. Hodge with Amy on his other side. Her right arm was sore, but ready to be raised.

Mr. Hodge stared at Meghan hard, looking angry. He broke the stare when he raised Amy's hand. Before Meghan could react, the coach from the MMA Academy bolted into the ring. "Hodge, what are you doing? Your girl won the fight."

"She didn't finish her, and your girl was the aggressor," Mr. Hodge said flatly.

Meghan and Amy looked at each other with a combination of confusion and sympathy. Mr. Hodge and the MMA Academy coach moved the discussion to the corner of the cage.

Amy took out her mouthpiece. "You won. Doesn't matter what the ref says."

When the MMA Academy coach left the ring, he appeared to be cursing under his breath. Mr. Hodge walked back in between Meghan and Amy. Again, he glared at Meghan.

"The decision stands," Mr. Hodge said as he raised Amy's hand. Meghan touched Amy's gloves and walked out of the cage. She stood by the door of the dojo and waited.

When Mr. Hodge arrived, she said nothing. He put his hand on Meghan's shoulder and the hard stare turned soft. He spoke quietly. "Next time, Megs, finish her like I know you can."

"I know, I know." She heard her mother's voice in her uncle's disappointment.

"If you weren't family... I mean, anyone else I'd boot from this dojo," Mr. Hodge said.

"Because I lost? You wouldn't have much of a dojo." Meghan laughed.

Mr. Hodge pressed harder on her shoulder. "I saw you over at the water fountain. You're not fooling anyone anymore. You'd better choose: are you going to be a champion or not?"

"Fooling anyone about what?" The words tumbled from her mouth.

"You were clean for a while after we went to Hawaii. Now you stay clean, or you leave my dojo. Got it?"

Now Meghan saw her mom's disappointment in Mr. Hodge's eyes too. He said nothing else, leaving Meghan in silence to weigh her decision.

CHAPTER 13

"So, how does it feel to be eighteen?" Meghan asked Hector at the small party she'd organized at Pizza Hut.

"No different, except I can vote and fight in the cage," Hector said. Hector would be the first of them to fight amateur, then Nong, Jackson, and finally Meghan.

"At eighteen you can enlist for military service," Jackson said. "I'm ready to go."

"Aren't you scared? I mean, what if you get sent off to war?" Meghan asked.

"That's what soldiers do; they fight wars.

They fight and die for their country."

"I think the only people I'd fight and die for are my family," Meghan said, sipping her soda.

Jackson shook his head, like he felt sad for her. He started to say something but got drawn into a UFC conversation with Nong and Hector's boss from the garage he worked at. Just as well, since Meghan knew sometimes people in your family died without a fight, or a reason.

"Hey, can I ask you something?" Hector whispered to Meghan. "Do you really believe what you said?"

Meghan responded with a puzzled look.

"You know, that the only people you would die for are your family."

"Of course, Hector. Don't you think your family would do anything for you?" Meghan asked, but Hector didn't answer. "It's all about sacrificing for what you love, you know? Look at us. We've surrendered years of our life to this. While other kids our age are out having a good time, we're in a gym getting beat up. And we like it. Not the pain, but the competition."

"Getting that W."

"Well, no, I don't know. If it was just about winning, all of us would've quit that first year when we were just human punching bags. Nong would've quit after getting killed last week. Yeah, we want to win, but it's the thrill of the fight itself, of taking on whatever strikes life throws your way. At least, it is for me." She looked up at Hector. "What is it for you?"

When Hector didn't have an answer, Meghan left the table. She walked slowly through the restaurant; the sounds of families laughing overwhelmed her with anger and sadness. She started to call Tommy, but stopped. Everyone in the dojo talked about how strong Meghan was. She knew it was time she proved them right.

◻ ◻ ◻ ◻ ◻ ◻

When Meghan arrived home, the pain grew more intense. Whatever damage the kicks had done to Amy, they'd hurt Meghan too. Her ankles throbbed. After an hour of craving rest, she caved and ventured downstairs. *You just need to get some sleep*, Meghan thought. *One pill, that's all.*

She stared at the pink pillbox for a long time before opening it and removing the small white pill. She tossed it back and felt relief at knowing sleep would come. Behind her, she heard a cough.

"What are you doing?" her grandfather asked. Meghan stood frozen, afraid to move. "Meghan, I don't want to believe what I just saw. Did you take one of our pills?"

Meghan moved in front of the counter with the pillbox, but didn't resist when her grandfather asked her to move aside. He opened his box first and then his wife's container.

He said nothing, just stared, his eyes a mix of shock and disappointment. It was too much for Meghan to ignore.

Latasha was right, Meghan thought, *it's all a hamster wheel.* Before she climbed into an MMA cage for a real fight, Meghan knew she needed to become human again.

"I'm so sorry," she managed to get out as the tears spilled over and Meghan ran up the stairs. For the first time since her mom's death, Meghan cried herself to sleep.

CHAPTER 14

"Are you insane?" Latasha asked seriously as she stepped through the door and into Meghan's home. The door, like the rest of the house, was decorated with "Happy 18th Birthday" signs. Unlike Hector's party, this one was for family and school friends. No fighters allowed.

"Why do you ask?" Meghan asked in return.

Latasha stared wide-eyed. "I heard that you invited Tommy to the party. What are you thinking?"

"Wait 'til Tommy gets here and I'll explain."

"I'm not sure I want to be here when she

gets here," Latasha said.

"No, you need to be here," Meghan said. She reached out and hugged Latasha. "And I need you to come to my first fight. I want Tommy there too. It would mean the world."

"Of course," Latasha answered. "Didn't I say it would be nice to finally meet some of your fighter friends? You've kept them so hidden from us. I assume none are here?"

Meghan paused and bit her lip.

"What's wrong?" Latasha asked. "Don't you want me to meet them?"

Another pause, another bite. "There's something about me that others in the dojo can't know yet," Meghan said quietly.

Latasha nodded. "About your mom?"

Meghan shook her head and pointed at her mom's brother. "No, about our dojo master. They don't know he's my uncle."

⬛ ⬛ ⬛ ⬛ ⬛ ⬛

Tommy crossed her arms. "So, what do you want to talk to me about?"

Meghan looked around the crowded room.

"Here, come outside," she said as she motioned for Tommy and Latasha to follow her out. Tommy and Latasha walked behind her without speaking to each other.

"What's going on?" Tommy asked when Meghan stopped and sat on the curb.

Meghan motioned for her two friends to sit down. Tommy sat a few feet away and pulled out a pack of cigarettes from her purse. Latasha stayed standing, arms crossed.

"It's my eighteenth birthday, so I guess I'm an adult," Meghan said. "But I feel like I have some unfinished business from my childhood—our childhood. I want to make peace between the three of us. It won't change anything that's happened, but I need for us to be right, okay?"

Both Latasha and Tommy nodded.

"Do you know why we were so good together?" Meghan asked. While the dojo was like a family, it wasn't a team sport. There was no sacrifice for the greater good.

"Because I was great." Tommy quipped. Then she lit the smoke. Latasha sighed deeply.

Meghan laughed. "We were good players,

but my mom made us great. She knew what each of us could do in basketball and volleyball. She knew our strengths and weaknesses."

"Your mom was a great coach," Latasha said. Meghan motioned again for her to sit. Latasha paused, then sat next to Meghan. "The best coach I've had."

"Our attack was balanced because we each did different things well," Meghan said.

"Remember the state championship game against Columbia East?" Latasha asked. Tommy and Meghan nodded as Latasha recounted the critical last minutes of the title game. Meghan closed her eyes and experienced it all again: Tommy's passes, Latasha's rebounds, her shots. She heard the roar of the crowd. She saw her mom's face explode in pride and delight.

"Those were the days," Tommy said. "Makes me sad."

"I thought it made me sad too," Meghan explained. "But mostly... mostly it makes me angry. Angry that everything we thought would happen in our lives got destroyed in just a matter of seconds. Like in MMA, you train for years, yet you could lose in an instant."

"It made me angry too, then sad, and then . . ." Tommy started to cry.

"Then it was easier not to feel anything at all," Latasha said.

"You sound so judgmental when you say it," Meghan said. "You don't know."

Latasha put her hand on Meghan's shoulder. "You're right. I'm sorry."

Meghan rubbed her hand over her stomach. Even through her clothing, she felt the outlines of the scars from the shattered glass and the operations. She looked at Latasha and Tommy's beautiful faces and hated every mirror in her house.

"I'm sorry we fought," Tommy said softly. "It all just makes me so angry."

"It's not fair," Latasha said. "I know that sounds childish, but it's true. That's what makes me angry. I mean, I get that the world is unfair, but—I don't know."

After a moment, Meghan spoke again. "Sometimes, I think the reason I fight is so I can get all that anger out, but it never really worked. I stayed angry and depressed, not to mention in pain."

"Well, you're always so medicated," Latasha said.

Latasha and Meghan looked at each other, then at Tommy. Tommy smoked instead of speaking. "So I'm clean now," Meghan continued. "It was hard, but I'm staying clean. You should try it, Tommy."

"No, thanks." Tommy laughed. "I'm happy for you, but I'm fine."

"You really want to be a pill head? High and low all the time?" Latasha asked.

"It's better than being angry or sad all the time. It makes my life easier," Tommy said. Meghan said nothing while Latasha and Tommy debated the merits of a medicated life. They talked back and forth, volleying Meghan's life choices like a ball across a net.

"Look," Meghan finally said. "When I'm sad, when I'm missing my mom, you know, I can get through it because I can balance that with the good times. I have so many good memories that kind of fill the holes." She paused. "But the anger, there's nothing to balance that. There's nothing to fill in for the loss, not just of her life, but in our lives. The loss of our future together. I could win every fight the rest of my life, and I don't think it would make a difference."

Tommy moved over closer. She put out her smoke and placed her arm on Meghan's shoulder. Latasha moved in close to them. They sat in silence.

Meghan bent over and touched her ankles. She ran her fingers across the zigzag scars on her face. Then she let the full weight of her head fall into her open palms. She squeezed her eyes shut tight, but this time she heard no roar of the crowd or her mother coaching from the bench. Instead, she heard two cars colliding. She felt the sharp pain of the shattering glass showering her body and her ankles crushed under the seat as the car rolled over and then came to rest on its side. She tasted blood in her mouth and smelled gasoline. But it was what she didn't hear that brought tears: she didn't hear her mom scream her name, or yell in pain, or even breathe. The silence was the loudest sound she'd ever heard. A silence she had shut out with pills and fought with punches. In the silence, Meghan's tears flowed. Her head was still down when sounds of sniffling broke the quiet and told her Tommy and Latasha were crying as well.

Once Meghan had stopped crying, Latasha said, "You know, it does make a difference if you win."

"To who?" Meghan asked.

Latasha looked upward. Tommy's eyes followed, and finally Meghan's.

"What was that thing your mom always told us, Meghan?" Tommy asked.

"You're not just athletes," Meghan said, "You're champions." It was time to prove it.

CHAPTER 15
TALE OF THE TAPE FOR FRIDAY NIGHT FIGHTS

WOMEN'S FEATHERWEIGHT	MEGHAN HODGE	JOSIE ROBERTS
AGE	18	18
HEIGHT	5' 8"	5' 9"
REACH	71"	73"
RECORD	0-0	0-0

CHAPTER 16

Meghan paced nervously outside the locker room before the weigh-in. Jackson stood with her for support along with Tyresha, a new girl at the dojo who Meghan saw as good future competition.

"You okay?" Tyresha asked Meghan. Jackson stood silent.

Meghan nodded.

"So what's your plan?" Tyresha asked.

"Knees in the clinch on top, arm bar on bottom, and body shots all over. You know, and the basics—use my speed, my strength, my training, and my memory."

"Your memory?"

"I've fought her before, I know what she has. But mostly I remember losing to her."

"I wonder what we'll remember more—the wins or the losses?" Tyresha asked.

Almost at the same time, Jackson and Meghan answered, "The losses."

◦ ◦ ◦ ◦ ◦ ◦

Before the fighter introductions, Meghan fought the urge to scan the crowd. She knew Latasha was there; she hoped Tommy was as well. But she also knew that Hector, Jackson, and others from the dojo were there, about to find out one of the secrets she had managed to keep from her dojo mates for so long. What they would think when the announcer introduced her?

"In this corner," the announcer said, "fighting out of the Missouri MMA dojo in her amateur debut, niece of local MMA legend Daniel Hodge, let's hear it for Meghan Hodge!"

Polite applause filled the arena. Mr. Hodge put his hand on Meghan's shoulder. "Good luck, Megs. Work hard and protect yourself."

"Don't worry," Meghan said, "I got this. I learned from the best." She flashed him a hint of a smile before double-checking her protective gear.

After Mr. Hodge left the cage, Meghan walked head-down to the center of the ring for the ref's instructions. Josie danced the entire time, while Meghan banged her gloves together. Meghan didn't need to see the smug look on Josie's face from their first battle. She didn't want to see Josie's face until she landed a fist, knee, or foot and smashed her smugness like a bug.

At the sound of the bell, the fighters touched gloves. Josie landed first with inside leg kicks, four of them to the left knee. Meghan answered with a leg kick of her own and a front kick that Josie blocked. Josie avoided another body shot and grabbed Meghan's leg. A quick heel trip put Meghan on her back, but she felt no panic. She knew it's what you did after the fall that mattered.

On the ground, Meghan quickly got full guard, shutting Josie down. When one of Josie's elbows missed, Meghan executed a sweep from underneath and stood. On their feet, the fighters circled and exchanged strikes until Josie tried another takedown. Meghan fought it off, clinched Josie's neck, and brought her knees up. But Josie escaped the clinch and moved back.

Meghan faked a high kick with her right leg. When Josie moved her arms to block the kick, Meghan buried a hard left hook into Josie's side. Even with the noise in the arena, Meghan heard the gasp of pain shoot from deep inside of Josie. Josie tried for an underhook, but Meghan was too quick. Getting her arms free, she found enough distance to bury four hard knees in rapid fire to Josie's side. Josie covered her right side—leaving her left exposed. Meghan got the distance she needed and exploded a rock-hard roundhouse kick to the soft flesh between Josie's ribs and hip. Josie dropped to one knee.

"Thirty seconds!"

Meghan rushed Josie, pushing her to the ground. As Josie rolled up on her head, bridging her neck to try to escape, she exposed her chin. Meghan crushed it with an uppercut. From the full mount, Meghan threw lefts at Josie's head but used her right to continue a rain of unanswered body shots. As she started to throw an overhand left, she felt the ref's arm on hers to stop the strike as the sound of the bell and the applause of the crowd filled her ears.

Meghan took off her headgear and threw it in the air, then bent down and helped Josie regain her feet. Josie stood as the announcer said, "Your winner, by TKO in the first round, Meghan Hodge." When the ref raised her hand, Meghan forced back tears.

⬛ ⬛ ⬛ ⬛ ⬛ ⬛

"Mr. Hodge is your uncle?" Tyresha asked Meghan as she left the ring. "That's wild."

Meghan nodded, but before she could say anything else, her uncle came up behind them. "Tyresha, don't blame Meghan. I told her that she couldn't let any of you know. And I have to say, for a teenage girl, she did a pretty good job of keeping it a secret for years."

"I have experience," Meghan mumbled.

Tyresha shot her a questioning look, but Meghan said nothing.

Mr. Hodge continued. "So you're okay with people knowing you're my niece now? Honestly?"

Meghan took a deep breath. "Honestly? I guess I'm relieved."

Mr. Hodge just nodded, his face hardening a bit. "Secrets control you and weigh you down, Megs."

Meghan said nothing to her uncle, but motioned for Tyresha to follow her toward the locker room.

"What's he talking about?" Tyresha asked once they were inside.

Meghan hesitated, but then stripped off her gear and pointed to the scars like snakes on her torso. "This, these scars and how I got them."

Tyresha shrugged and squinted. "For serious?" She shrugged. "Meghan, you can barely see them. Like the tiny ones on your face—Jackson told me. I didn't notice until then. Besides, anybody who goes through life without scars ain't lived."

"I know something about that," Meghan said as she headed to the showers and stepped under the water. She could feel the weight ready to be lifted.

Once she stepped out of the locker room, they were all there to congratulate her—her dojo mates, Latasha, and Tommy. Meghan laughed at how eager Latasha was to meet the others as Hector threw questions at Meghan about her fight. After a round of introductions, Meghan and Latasha made plans to meet up later, and Tommy and Latasha took off.

When only the other dojo fighters were left, Meghan asked everybody to sit on the floor of the gym. She wasn't sure if the setting was right, but the time was.

"So what's up, Miss Hodge?" Nong asked with a smile.

"Okay, so now you guys know why I practically live at the dojo," Meghan started. "I guess I want you to know about my scars too."

Meghan told her dojo mates about her mom and the accident. She exposed her stomach and then pulled up her pant legs to show the marks it had left. But the scars on her torso and ankles that once seemed huge didn't seem quite so bad anymore. Just like with Tyresha, nobody recoiled in horror. Surveying their reactions,

Meghan wondered if she'd hidden herself for no reason other than her own fears.

As she talked with her training partners, Meghan felt like she'd won a close fight by decision. She had taken a beating, and the scars from it would remain. But one day, she knew, the pain would wash away. And she would be left a champion.

APPENDIX
MMA TERMS

Brazilian jiu-jitsu (BJJ): a martial art that focuses on grappling, in particular fighting on the ground; also called Gracie jiu-jitsu

choke: any hold used by a fighter around an opponent's throat with the goal of submission. A blood choke cuts off the supply of blood to the brain, while an air choke restricts oxygen. Types of choke holds include rear naked (applied from behind), guillotine (applied from in front), and triangle (applied from the ground).

dojo: a Japanese term meaning "place of the way," once used for temples but now more commonly used for gyms or schools where martial arts are taught

guard: a position on the mat where the fighter on his or her back uses his or her body to guard against an opponent's offensive moves by controlling the foe's body

jiu-jitsu: a Japanese-based martial art that uses no weapons and focuses less on strikes and more on grappling

Kimura: a judo submission hold. Its technical name is ude-garami, but it is usually referred to by the name of its inventor, Japanese judo master Masahiko Kimura.

mount: a dominant position where one fighter is on the ground and the other is on top

Muay Thai: a martial art from Thailand using striking and clinches. It is often referred to as the art of eight limbs for its use of right and left knees, fists, elbows, and feet.

pass guard: when the fighter on top escapes from the controlling guard position of the fighter on bottom

shoot: in amateur wrestling, to attempt to take an opponent down

sprawl: a strategy to avoid takedowns by shooting the legs back or moving away from a foe

submission: any hold used to end a fight when one fighter surrenders (taps out) because the hold causes pain or risk of injury

sweep: when a fighter reverses position from being on the ground or in the guard to being on top or in the mount

takedown: an offensive move to take an opponent to the mat. Takedowns include single leg, double leg, and underhooks.

tap: the motion a fighter uses to show he or she is surrendering. A fighter can tap either the mat or the opponent with a hand.

TKO: technical knockout. A fighter who is not knocked out but can no longer defend himself or herself is "technically" knocked out, and the referee will stop the fight.

UFC: Ultimate Fighting Championship, the largest, most successful mixed martial arts promotion in the world since its beginning in 1993

underhook: a takedown executed by one fighter hooking his or her arms under the opponent's arms and using that leverage to throw the opponent to the ground

MMA WEIGHT CLASSES

Flyweight	under 125.9 pounds
Bantamweight	126–134.9 pounds
Featherweight	135–144.9 pounds
Lightweight	145–154.9 pounds
Welterweight	155–169.9 pounds
Middleweight	170–184.9 pounds
Light Heavyweight	185–204.9 pounds
Heavyweight	205–264.9 pounds
Super Heavyweight	over 265 pounds

WELCOME TO

THE DOJO

BODY SHOT
PATRICK JONES

HEAD KICK
PATRICK JONES

SIDE CONTROL
PATRICK JONES

TRIANGLE CHOKE
PATRICK JONES

LEARN TO FIGHT, LEARN TO LIVE, AND LEARN TO FIGHT FOR YOUR LIFE.

SOUTHSIDE HIGH

ARE YOU A SURVIVOR?

Check out all the books in the

SURVIVING SOUTH SIDE

collection

ABOUT THE AUTHOR

Patrick Jones is the author of numerous novels for teens, including the Dojo series, as well as the nonfiction books *The Main Event: The Moves and Muscle of Pro Wrestling* and *Ultimate Fighting: The Brains and Brawn of Mixed Martial Arts* from Millbrook Press. A former librarian for teenagers, he received a lifetime achievement award from the American Library Association in 2006. He lives in Minneapolis but still considers Flint, Michigan, his hometown. He can be found on the web at www.connectingya.com and in front of his TV most weekends, watching UFC and WWE pay-per-views.